j398.8 Mother Goose.

To market! To market!

C1

DATE DUE

FEB 0 7 1998	
SEP 2 2 1998	
APR 0 4 1999	
MAY 1 4 1999	
DEC 0 3 1999	
NOV 0 2 2000	
MAR 0 6 2003	
DEC 1 9 2006	

GAYLORD   PRINTED IN U.S.A.

© THE BAKER & TAYLOR CO.

THE MOTHER GOOSE LIBRARY

THE MOTHER GOOSE LIBRARY

This one is for Kathy!

To Market! To Market!

The Mother Goose Library

Birds of a feather flock together,
And so will pigs and swine;
Rats and mice will have their choice,
And so will I have mine.

To Market! To Market!

Illustrated by Peter Spier

Doubleday & Company, Inc.

Garden City, New York

Library of Congress Catalog Card Number 67-18664. Copyright © 1967 by Peter Spier. All Rights Reserved. Printed in the United States of America.

9 8 7 6 5 4 3 C1

Cocks crow in the morn
To tell us to rise,
For he who lies late
Will never be wise;
For early to bed and early to rise,
Makes a man healthy,
    and wealthy, and wise.

He that would thrive
Must rise at five;
He that has thriven
May lie till seven;
And he that will never thrive
May lie till eleven.

Elsie Marley is grown so fine, She won't get up to feed the swine,

But lies in bed till eight or nine. Lazy Elsie Marley.

The Cock: Lock the dairy door,
    Lock the dairy door.
The Hen: Chickle, chackle, chee,
    I haven't got the key.

The cock's on the house-top,
Blowing his horn;
The bull's in the barn,
A-threshing the corn;
The maids in the meadow
Are making the hay;
The ducks in the river
Are swimming away.

I had a little cow and to save her,
I turned her into the meadow to graze her;

There came a heavy storm of rain,
And drove the little cow home again.

The church doors they stood open,
And there the little cow was cropen;

Erected by
B
A

Sacred to the

Reader Since Minutes
Fly in Hast, Improve
Ye Present As Thy Last.

Elizabeth Hind, Wife
of Tho: E Bird Born in
Liverpool. GB. Oct 2 1687

She dyed Sep.t 1st.
Anno Domini 1725 Ae 38 Yrs.

AF
1782

1803

Ths. H.

2 16

73

81

The bell-ropes they were made of hay,
And the little cow ate them all away;

The sexton came to toll the bell,
And pushed the little cow into the well!

Four stiff-standers,
Four dilly-danders,
Two lookers, two crookers,
And a wig-wag.

Cushy cow, bonny, let down thy milk,
And I will give thee a gown of silk;
A gown of silk and a silver tee,
If thou wilt let down thy milk to me.

A whistling girl and a flock of sheep

Are two good things for a farmer to keep.

Father and Mother and Uncle John
Went to the market one by one;

Father fell off —!

Mother fell off —!

But Uncle John went on, and on,

And on, and on, and on.

This little pig went to market,

This little pig stayed home,

This little pig had roast beef,

And this little pig had none,

And this little pig went wee-wee-wee

All the way home.

To market, to market, to buy a fat pig,

Home again, home again, jiggety-jig.

Barber, barber, shave a pig,
How many hairs to make a wig?
Four and twenty, that's enough,
Give the farmer a pinch of snuff.

To market, to market, to buy a fat hog,
Home again, home again, jiggety-jog.

If a man who turnips cries,
Cry not when his father dies,
It is proof that he would rather
Have a turnip than his father.

Robert Barnes, fellow fine,
Can you shoe this horse of mine?
Yes, good sir, that I can,
As well as any other man.
There's a nail, and there's a prod,
And now, good sir, your horse is shod.

Cheese and bread for gentlemen,
Corn and hay for horses,
Tobacco for the auld wives,
And kisses for the lasses.

Little maid, little maid, where have you been?
I've been to see grandmother over the green.
What did she give you? Milk in a can.
What did you say for it? Thank you, Grandam.

To market, to market, to buy a plum bun,

Home again, home again, market is done!

This is silver Saturday,
The morn's the resting day:
Monday up and to it again,
And Tuesday push away.

Some five miles south of Wilmington, Delaware, on the west bank of the Delaware River, is the town of old New Castle, now sleepy and picturesque, but once a busy seaport and market town of the new nation of the United States.

Delaware was first settled by the Swedes and the Finns in 1638. In 1651, the irascible Pieter Stuyvesant took over for the Dutch, named the town New Amstel, and built Fort Casimir.

Under Dutch rule New Amstel was the market town for both the European settlers and the Indians. Pieter Stuyvesant himself is said to have laid out the plan of the streets, the Market Place, and the Green. The site of Fort Casimir has now disappeared into the river, but one may still see Old Dutch House, at least a part of which dates back to those days.

Life in the 17th-century settlement, however, was not peaceful. For 30 years control of the town passed back and forth amongst the Swedes, the Dutch, and finally the English who renamed the town New Castle, probably for Newcastle-on-Tyne. At least a part of the present Court House dates back to this time, making it the oldest public building in America.

In 1682 William Penn took title to the territory, but in 1704 the settlers of Delaware, chafing under Penn's rule, set up the separate Assembly of Delaware at New Castle.

Now came a period of growth and prosperity. New Castle blossomed with fine houses and buildings, many of which, such as the Amstel House and Booth House survive today. The present Immanuel Church (where "the little cow was cropen" and ate the bellropes) was begun in 1703, though its churchyard (down the non-existent well of which the cow was pushed) did not open until 1791. In 1730 the Assembly decreed that on the Wednesday and Saturday market days no food except fish, milk, and bread might be sold anywhere else in town than at the Market Place. The central part of the Court House was built in 1732; still later the cupola was added, said to be the mathematical center for the arc forming the northern boundary of Delaware.

The issues of the American Revolution were hotly debated in Assembly, but as the war went on the seat was moved to Dover for fear of British attack. Prudent though the move may have been, it began the decline of New Castle's importance.

In the early 1800's New Castle had a brief renaissance when it was the transfer point between coastal sailing packets and the overland stages across the peninsula to the

Chesapeake. In 1831, too, the New Castle and French-town Railroad put into service the first, regularly scheduled steam engine, with its terminus at what is today the Town Hall (the square building on the Market Place with an archway through it). Some of its old tracks are still visible.

In this book Peter Spier has conjured up the New Castle of the early 19th century—let us say 1828. He made many trips through Delaware, Maryland, and Pennsylvania sketching and collecting details for the book. Many of his illustrations are accurate renditions of what a visitor to New Castle today might see. But some of them are that synthesis of actual, present-day detail and reconstruction of "how it must have been" that is the special province of an artist.

The cobble-stoned Strand, on which Mr. Spier has situated the barber shop where the pig was shaved, is still to be seen. Packet Alley, down which the farmer rides home from market, is still there, though the wharves are ruined. But the barber shop and the house on the other side of Packet Alley are composites of typical houses of the town. The Marley farm does not exist, although it is made up of elements from a dozen or more barnyards and farmhouses which Mr. Spier sketched.

Probably, too, the farm was nearer to the New Castle Fair than the Brandywine powdermills which were built

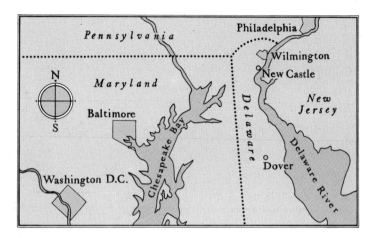

in the early 1800's by the first DuPonts, but the mill which Mr. Spier used as a background for the dunking of the Marley family is today a part of the Hagley Museum.

During the 19th century New Castle lay in its backwater, outstripped by Dover to the south and Wilmington to the north, comfortably sheltered from the "progress" which might have rebuilt the waterfront and cleared away the old houses. In recent years the residents of Old New Castle, some of them descendants of colonial townspeople, have made great strides in the restoration and preservation of this historic spot. And today, every year on the third Saturday in May, they open their houses and their town to visitors so that they may catch a glimpse of days gone by.

THE MOTHER GOOSE LIBRARY

THE MOTHER GOOSE LIBRARY

In 1952 Peter Spier came to New York from Amsterdam, where he was born and educated. Since that time he has established himself as one of this country's most gifted young illustrators, with a number of books to his credit. Among them are *The Cow Who Fell in the Canal* by Phyllis Krasilovsky, for which his native Holland provided the background, and *Wonder Tales of Seas and Ships* by Frances Carpenter, a subject familiar to him through his service with the Royal Dutch Navy.

In 1962, Peter Spier illustrated the perennial favorite folk song entitled, *The Fox Went Out on a Chilly Night,* which was a runner-up for the Caldecott Medal. The delightful period setting of *The Fox* is the result of a trip through New England during which he sketched old houses, barns, covered bridges, and the lovely autumn countryside.

Since then he has been involved with the development and production of a series of twenty-four books, of which he illustrated seven. Mr. Spier is married and lives with his wife and children in Port Washington, Long Island.